PUFFIN BOOKS

A Narrow Squeak and Other Animal Stories

Dick King-Smith served in the Grenadier Guards during the Second World War, and afterwards spent twenty years as a farmer in Gloucestershire, the county of his birth. Many of his stories are inspired by his farming experiences. Later he taught at a village primary school. His first book, *The Fox Busters*, was published in 1978. Since then he has written a great number of children's books, including *The Sheep-Pig* (winner of the *Guardian* Award and filmed as *Babe*), *Harry's Mad, Noah's Brother, The Hodgeheg, Martin's Mice, Ace, The Cuckoo Child* and *Harriet's Hare* (winner of the Children's Book Award in 1995). At the British Book Awards in 1992 he was voted Children's Author of the Year. He is married, with three children and eleven grandchildren, and lives in a seventeenth-century cottage a short crow's-flight from the house where he was born.

DICK KING-SMITH

A Narrow Squeak and Other Animal Stories

Illustrated by Amanda Harvey

PUFFIN BOOKS

PUFFIN BOOKS

Published by the Penguin Group
Penguin Books Ltd, 27 Wrights Lane, London W8 5TZ, England
Penguin Putnam Inc., 375 Hudson Street, New York, New York 10014, USA
Penguin Books Australia Ltd, Ringwood, Victoria, Australia
Penguin Books Canada Ltd, 10 Alcorn Avenue, Toronto, Ontario, Canada M4V 3B2
Penguin Books (NZ) Ltd, Private Bag 102902, NSMC, Auckland, New Zealand

On the World Wide Web at: www.penguin.com

Penguin Books Ltd, Registered Offices: Harmondsworth,
Middlesex, England

First published by Viking 1993
Published in Puffin Books 1995
8

The moral right of the author and illustrator has been asserted

Set in Monophoto Garamond

Made and printed in England by Clays Ltd, St Ives plc

British Library Cataloguing in Publication Data
A CIP catalogue record for this book is available from
the British Library

ISBN 0–140–34963–4

Contents

A Narrow Squeak

'Do you realize,' said Ethel, 'that tomorrow is our Silver Wedding Day?'

'So soon?' said Hedley in a surprised voice. 'How time flies! Why, it seems but yesterday that we were married.'

'Well, it isn't,' said Ethel sharply. 'You only have to look at me to see that.'

Hedley looked at her.

She seems to have put on a great deal of weight, he thought. Not that she isn't still by far the most beautiful mouse in the world, of course, but there's a lot more of her now.

'You have certainly grown,' he said tactfully.

'Grown?' snapped Ethel. 'And whose fault is that, pray? Anyone would think you didn't know why I'm blown out like a balloon. Goodness knows what sort of a father you will make.'

'A father?' said Hedley. 'You mean . . .?'

'Any time now,' said Ethel. 'And I'm starving hungry, Hedley. Fetch us something nice to eat, do. I could just fancy something savoury.'

She sighed deeply as her husband hurried away. Was there ever such a mouse, she said to herself. *So* handsome, but so *thick*. Let's hope he doesn't walk straight down the cat's throat. I wouldn't put it past him, and then there won't be any

Silver Wedding.

A mouse's life is, of course, a short one, fraught with hazards. For those that survive their childhood, Death looms in many shapes and forms, among them the cat, the poison bait and the trap, and mice have learned to commemorate anniversaries in good time. 'Better early than never' is a favourite mouse proverb, and Ethel and Hedley's Silver Wedding was to be celebrated twenty-five days after their marriage.

If they were lucky, they would go on to a Pearl, a Ruby, a Golden, and, should they be spared to enjoy roughly two months of wedded bliss, to a Diamond Wedding Anniversary. Beyond that, no sensible mouse cared to think.

If only Hedley was more sensible, Ethel thought as she lay, uncomfortably on account of the pressure within her, in her nest. Not that he isn't still by far the most beautiful mouse in the world, of course, but he's so accident-prone.

Hardly a day passed when Ethel did not hear, somewhere about the house, a thin cry of alarm, indicating that Hedley had just had a narrow squeak.

He goes about in a dream, she said to herself. He doesn't *think*. Surely other mice didn't stand in the path of vacuum cleaners, or explore inside tumble-driers, or come close to drowning in a bowl of cat's milk?

In fact, Hedley was thinking quite hard as he emerged from the hole in the skirting-board that was the entrance to their home, and prepared to make his way across the kitchen floor.

'A father!' he murmured happily to himself. 'I am to be a father! And soon! How many children will there be, I wonder? How many will be boys, how many girls? And what shall we call them? What fun it will be, choosing the names!'

This was what Ethel had meant when she said that Hedley did not think. Her

thoughts were very practical and filled
with common sense, and she was quick
to make up her mind. By contrast, Hedley
was a day-dreamer and much inclined to
be absent-minded when, as now, he was
following up an idea.

He had just decided to call his eldest
son Granville after a favourite uncle,
when he bumped into something soft and
furry, something that smelt, now that he
came to think of it, distinctly unpleasant.

The cat, fast asleep in front of the

Aga cooker, did not wake, but it twitched
its tail.

With a shrill cry, Hedley ran for
cover. The larder door was ajar, and he
slipped in and hid behind a packet of
Corn Flakes.

The noise he had made reached
Ethel's ears, and filled her mind, as so
often over the previous twenty-four days,
with thoughts of widowhood. It also
woke the cat, who rose, stretched and
padded towards the larder.

'Not in there, puss!' said its owner, coming into her kitchen, and she shut the larder door.

Hedley was a prisoner.

For some time he crouched motionless. As happened after such frights, his mind was a blank. But gradually his thoughts returned to those unborn children. The eldest girl, now – what was she to be called?

After a while Hedley decided upon Dulcibel, his grandmother's name. But then suppose Ethel did not agree? Thinking of Ethel reminded him of her last words. 'Fetch us something nice to eat, do,' she had said. 'I could just fancy something savoury.'

Hedley raised his snout and sniffed.

This little room, in which he had never been before, certainly smelt of all kinds of food, and this reminded him that he was himself a bit peckish. He began to explore the larder, climbing up on to its shelves and running about to see what he could find. I'll have a snack, he said to himself, to keep me going, and then I'll find something really nice to take back to Ethel.

Much of the food in the larder was in cans or packets, but Hedley found a slab of fruit cake and some butter in a dish and a plate of cold chips. At last, feeling full, he hid behind a row of tins and settled down for a nap.

Meanwhile, back at the nest, Ethel was growing increasingly uneasy. He must have had his chips, she thought, and our children will be born fatherless. She was hungry, she was uncomfortable, and she was more and more worried that Hedley had not returned.

'Oh Hedley, how I shall miss you!' she breathed. '*So* handsome, but so *thick*.'

While Hedley was sleeping off his huge meal, the larder door was opened.

'Just look at this cake!' a woman's

voice said. 'And these leftover chips! And the butter – little footmarks all over it! We've got mice.'

'Put the cat in there,' said a man's voice.

'Can't do that or it'll be helping itself too.'

'Well, set a trap then. And put some poison down.'

And a little later, the larder door was closed again.

Hedley slept the whole night through. He dreamed of happy times to come. In his dream, his handsome sons and his beautiful daughters had grown old enough to leave the nest, and he was taking them on

a conducted tour of the house. Then boldly he led them all, Granville and Dulcibel and the rest, and their mother too, through the cat-flap and out into the garden. 'For we will picnic,' he said to them, 'in the strawberry bed. The fruit is ripe and the weather exceedingly pleasant.'

'Oh Papa!' the children cried. 'What fun that will be!'

'But are you not afraid of the cat, Hedley dear?' said Ethel nervously.

'Ethel, Ethel,' said Hedley. 'When have you ever known me afraid of anything?' and the children chorused, 'Oh, brave Papa!' . . .

He woke from his dream with a number of other possible names for the impending family in mind – Eugene, Tallulah, Hereward and Morwenna were four that he particularly fancied – when he suddenly remembered with a sharp pang of guilt that Ethel was still unfed.

I shall get the rough edge of her tongue, he thought, and he looked about for a tasty item of food, small enough for him to carry.

He climbed down to a lower shelf and found something which had not, he was sure, been there before.

It was a saucer containing a number of little blue pellets, and beside it there was an opened packet. Had Hedley been able to read, he would have seen that on the packet was written:

MOUSE POISON, KEEP AWAY FROM
DOMESTIC ANIMALS

As it was, thinking how unusual and attractive the blue pellets looked, he took a mouthful of them. She'll love these, he thought, such a pretty colour, and he ran down to the floor of the larder only to find the door shut. Bother, thought Hedley. How am I to get out of this place?

He was considering this problem in a half-hearted way, for part of his mind was still occupied with names – would Annabel be better than Morwenna? – when his nose caught a most exciting smell. It was cheese, a little square lump of it, conveniently placed on a low shelf.

The cheese was in fact on a little wooden platform, an odd-looking thing that had a metal arm and a spring attached to it, but Hedley, busy deciding that after

all he preferred Morwenna, did not stop to think about this. It's Ethel's favourite food, he said to himself, and just the right size for me to carry back, and he spat out the little blue pellets and ran to grab the cheese.

Whether it was his speed or whether the trap had not been lightly enough set, Hedley got away with it.

SNAP! went the trap, missing him (though not by a whisker for it cut off three of them), and Hedley gave, through his mouthful of cheese, a muffled squeak of fright.

'Listen!' said the woman's voice, and 'You got him!' said the man's, and the larder door was opened.

For once Hedley did not day-dream. He streaked across the kitchen floor and into his hole, the lump of cheese clenched in his jaws.

Ethel regarded him silently from the nest.

Hedley dropped his burden before her.

'Sorry I'm late,' he panted. 'I got held up. Here, it's Farmhouse Cheddar, your favourite. How have you been?'

'Busy,' said Ethel shortly.

'Busy?' said Hedley.

'Yes,' said Ethel.

She attacked the cheese hungrily, while Hedley lay and got his breath back. Funny, he thought, she looks slimmer than she did yesterday. As slim, in fact, as the day we met, and what a meeting that was! I remember it as though it were yesterday . . .

'Hedley!' said Ethel now, licking her lips as she finished the cheese. 'You do know what day it is, don't you?'

'Wednesday, I think,' said Hedley. 'Or it may be Thursday. I'm not sure.'

'Hedley,' said Ethel. 'It is our Silver Wedding Day.'

'Oh!' cried Hedley. 'I quite forgot.'

Typical, thought Ethel. He'd forget his head if it wasn't screwed on.

'I have a present for you,' she said, and she rose and stood aside from the nest.

In the middle of a comfortable, warm bed, made out of flock from a chair lining, and feathers from an eiderdown, and a mass of newspaper scraps, lay six fat, pink, naked babies.

'Three boys and three girls,' she said. 'Neat, eh?'

Oh! thought Hedley. What could be neater! Granville and Dulcibel, Eugene and Tallulah, and Hereward and Morwenna.

'Oh, Ethel dearest,' he said. 'I have no present for you but my love.'

At these words Ethel's annoyance melted away. What a fine-looking mouse he still is, she thought, not a grey hair on him. In fact, he looks no older than he did at our wedding, twenty-five long days ago.

Hedley sat in a daze, gazing at the babies.

Then he said, 'Oh Ethel! To think that you did this all on your own! You're so *clever*!'

And you're so *thick*, thought Ethel fondly, but out loud she said, 'Oh Hedley, you are *so* handsome!'

The Excitement of Being Ernest

The first thing that struck you about Ernest was his colour. If you had to put a name to it, you would say 'honey' – not that pale wax honey that needs a knife to get it out of a jar, but the darker, richer, runny stuff that drips all over the table-cloth if you don't wind the spoon round it properly.

That was the colour of Ernest's coat, and the second thing about him that was remarkable was the amount of coat he carried. He was very hairy. Body, legs, tail, all had their fair share of that runny-honey-coloured hair, but it was Ernest's face that was his fortune, with its fine beard and moustaches framed by shortish, droopy ears. From under bushy eyebrows, Ernest looked out upon the world and found it good. Only one thing bothered him. He did not know what kind of dog he was.

It should have been simple, of course, to find out. There were a number of other dogs living in the village who could presumably have told him, but somehow Ernest had never plucked up the courage to ask. To begin with, the other dogs all looked so posh. They were all of different breeds, but each one appeared so obviously well bred, so self-assured, so upper class, that Ernest had always hesitated to approach them, least of all with a daft question like, 'Excuse me. I wonder if you could tell me what sort of dog I am?'

For that matter, he thought to himself one day, I don't even know what sort of dogs they are, and then it occurred to him that that would be a much more sensible question to ask and could lead perhaps to the kind of conversation about breeds in general where one of them might say, 'I'm a Thingummytite, and you, I see, are a Wotchermecallum.'

So after he had helped to get the cows in for morning milking on the farm where he lived, Ernest trotted up to the village to the gateway of the Manor House – an imposing entrance flanked by fine pillars – and peered in under his bushy eyebrows. Standing in the drive was the Manor House dog. Ernest lifted his leg politely on one of the fine stone pillars, and called out, 'Excuse me! I wonder if you could tell me what sort of dog you are?'

'Ich bin ein German Short-haired

Pointer,' said the Manor House dog, 'if dot is any business of yours.'

'Oh,' said Ernest. 'I'm not one of those.'

He waited expectantly to be told what he was.

'Dot,' said the German Short-haired Pointer pointedly, 'is as plain as der nose on your face,' and he turned his back and walked away.

Ernest went on to the Vicarage, and saw, through the wicket-gate, the Vicar's dog lying on the lawn.

'Excuse me,' said Ernest, lifting his leg politely on the wicket-gate. 'I wonder if you could tell me what sort of dog you are?'

'Nom d'un chien!' said the Vicar's dog. 'Je suis un French Bulldog.'

'Oh,' said Ernest. 'I'm not one of those.'

The French Bulldog snorted, and though Ernest waited hopefully for a while, it said nothing more, so he walked down the road till he came to the pub.

The publican's dog was very large indeed, and Ernest thought it best to keep some distance away. He lifted his leg discreetly on an empty beer barrel and shouted across the pub car-park, 'Excuse me! I wonder if you could tell me what sort of dog you are?'

'Oi'm an Irish Wolfhound,' said the publican's dog in a deep, rumbly voice.

'Oh,' said Ernest. 'I'm not one of those.'

'Bedad you're not,' said the Irish Wolfhound. 'Shall Oi be after tellin' yez what sort of a dog ye are?'

'Oh, yes please,' said Ernest eagerly.

'Sure ye're a misbegotten hairy mess,' said the Irish Wolfhound, 'and it's stinking of cow-muck ye are. Now bate it, if ye know what's good for you.'

Ernest beat it. But he wasn't beaten.

He paid a call on a number of houses in the village street, repeating his polite inquiry and receiving answers of varying degrees of rudeness from a Tibetan Terrier, an American Cocker Spaniel, a Finn-nd a Chinese Crested Dog. But none of them volunteered any information as to what kind of animal he himself was.

There was one house left, by the junction of the road with the lane that led back to the farm, and standing outside it was a dog that Ernest had never seen before in the neighbourhood. It looked friendly and wagged its long, plumy tail as Ernest left his customary calling-card on the gate.

'Hello,' he said. 'I haven't seen you before.'

'We've only just moved in,' said the friendly stranger. 'You're the first dog I've met here, actually. Are there a lot in the village?'

'Yes.'

'Decent bunch?'

Ernest considered how best to answer this.

'They're all very well bred,' he said. 'I imagine they've got pedigrees as long as your tail,' he added, 'like you have, I suppose?'

'You could say that,' replied the other. 'For what it's worth.'

Ernest sighed. I'll give it one more go, he thought.

'Straight question,' he said. 'What sort of dog are you?'

'Straight answer, English Setter.'

'English?' said Ernest delightedly. 'Well, that makes a change.'

'How do you mean?'

'Why, the rest of them are Chinese, German, Tibetan, Irish, American, Finnish – there's no end to the list.'

'Really? No, no I'm as English as you are.'

'Ah,' said Ernest carefully. 'Then you know what sort of dog I am?'

'Of course,' said the English Setter. 'You're a Gloucestershire Cow-dog.'

The hair over Ernest's face prevented

the Setter from seeing the changing expression that flitted across it, first of astonishment, then of excitement, and finally a studied look of smug satisfaction.

'Ah,' said Ernest. 'You knew. Not many do.'

'My dear chap,' said the Setter. 'You amaze me. I should have thought any dog would have recognized a Gloucestershire Cow-dog immediately.'

'Really?' said Ernest. 'Well, I suppose any English dog would.'

'Yes, that must be it. Anyway you'll be able to compete with all these pedigree chaps next week.'

'Why, what's happening next week?'

'It's the Village Fête.'

'Oh, I don't go to that sort of thing,' said Ernest. 'I've got too much work to do with the cows.'

'Quite. But this year there's a new attraction, apparently. They've just put the posters up, haven't you seen?'

'Didn't notice,' said Ernest.

'Well, there's one stuck on our wall. Come and have a look.'

And this is what they saw.

VILLAGE FÊTE
Saturday June 15th
By kind permission, in the grounds
of the Manor House

Skittle Alley
Coconut Shy
Cake Stall
Jam and Preserve Stall
White Elephant Stall
Hoopla
Wellie-throwing Competition
Guess the Weight of the Pig
Grand Dog Show

'But that's no good,' said Ernest. 'With all the pedigree dogs in the village, the judge will never look twice at me.'

'But that's no good,' said Sally. 'With all the pedigree dogs in the village, the judge will never look twice at Ernest.' Sally was the farmer's daughter, and she was looking at another of the notices, tacked on the farm gate.

'Oh, I don't know,' said her father. 'You might be surprised. Have a go. It's only a bit of fun. You'll have to clean him up a bit, mind.'

So when the great day dawned, Ernest ran to Sally's whistle after morning milking and found himself, to his surprise and disgust, required to stand in an old tin bath and be soaked and lathered and scrubbed and hosed, and then blow-dried with Sally's mother's electric drier plugged in to a power point in the dairy.

'He looks a treat,' said the farmer and his wife when Sally had finished combing out that long, honey-coloured coat. And he did.

Indeed when they all arrived at the Fête, a number of people had difficulty in recognizing Ernest without his usual covering of cow-muck. But the dogs weren't

fooled. Ernest heard them talking among themselves as the competitors began to gather for the Dog Show, and their comments made his head drop and his tail droop.

'Well I'll be goshdarned!' said the American Cocker Spaniel to the Tibetan Terrier. 'Will ya look at that mutt! Kinda tough to have to share a show-ring with no-account trash like that.'

And, turning to the Finnish Spitz, 'Velly distlessing,' said the Chinese Crested Dog. 'No pediglee.'

'Ma foi!' said the French Bulldog to the Irish Wolfhound. 'Regardez zis 'airy creature! 'E is, 'ow you say, mongrel?'

'Begorrah, it's the truth ye're spakin,' said the Irish Wolfhound in his deep, rumbly voice, 'and it's stinking of soap powder he is.'

As for the German Short-haired Pointer, he made sure, seeing that he was host for the day, that his comment on Ernest's arrival on the croquet lawn

(which was the show-ring) was heard by all.

'Velcome to der Manor, ladies and gentlemen,' he said to the other dogs. 'May der best-bred dog win,' and he turned his back on Ernest in a very pointed way.

'Don't let them get you down, old chap,' said a voice in Ernest's ear, and there, standing next to him, was the friendly English Setter, long, plumy tail wagging.

'Oh, hello,' said Ernest in a doleful voice. 'Nice to see you. I hope you win, anyway. I haven't got a chance.'

'Oh, I don't know,' said the English Setter. 'You might be surprised. Have a go. It's only a bit of fun.'

He lowered his voice. 'Take a tip though, old chap. Don't lift your leg. It's not done.'

Suddenly Ernest felt much happier. He gave himself a good shake, and then when they all began to parade around the ring, he stepped out smartly at Sally's side, his long (clean) honey-coloured coat shining in the summer sunshine.

The judge examined each entry in turn, looking in their mouths, feeling their legs and their backs, studying them from all angles, and making them walk up and down, just as though it was a class in a Championship Show.

When her turn came, he said to Sally, 'What's your dog called?'

'Ernest.'

From under bushy eyebrows, Ernest looked out upon the judge.

'Hello, Ernest,' the judge said, and then hesitated, because there was one thing that bothered him. He did not know what kind of dog Ernest was.

'You don't see many of these,' he said to Sally.

'Oh yes you do. There are lots about.'

'Lots of . . .?'

'Gloucestershire Cow-dogs.'

'Of course, of course,' said the judge.

When he had carefully examined all the entries, he made them walk round once more, and then he called out the lady of the Manor with her German Short-haired Pointer. When they came eagerly forward, trying not to look too smug, he said, 'I've finished with you, thank you.'

And he called out, one after another, the Chinese Crested Dog and the Tibetan Terrier and the American Cocker Spaniel and the French Bulldog and the Irish Wolfhound and, to finish with, the Finnish Spitz, and said to each in turn, 'I've finished with you, thank you.'

Until the only dogs left on the croquet lawn were the English Setter and Ernest.

And the judge looked thoughtfully at both of them for quite a time before he straightened up and spoke to the owner of the English Setter.

'A very close thing,' he said, 'but I'm giving the first prize to the

Gloucestershire Cow-dog,' and he walked across to the Vicar whose job it was to make all the announcements on the public address system.

'Well done, old boy,' said the English Setter. 'It couldn't have happened to a nicer chap.'

'But I don't understand,' said Ernest. 'How could I have won? Against all you aristocratic fellows that are registered with the Kennel Club, and have lots of champions in your pedigrees?'

'Listen,' said the English Setter as the Tannoy began to crackle and the voice of the Vicar boomed across the gardens of the Manor House.

'Ladies and gentlemen! We have the result of our Grand Dog Show! It's not quite like Crufts, ha, ha — we do things a bit differently down here — and in our Show there has been only one class, for The Most Lovable Dog. And the winner is . . . Ernest, the Gloucestershire Cowdog!'

And Sally gave Ernest a big hug, and the judge gave Sally a little cup, and the English Setter wagged his plumy tail like mad, and everybody clapped like billy-o, and Ernest barked and barked so loudly that he must have been heard by nearly every cow in Gloucestershire.

Oh, the excitement of being Ernest!

Norty Boy

Hylda was an old-fashioned sort of animal. She did not hold with the free and easy ways of the modern hedgehog, and even preferred to call herself by the old name of 'hedgepig'. She planned to bring up her seven hedgepiglets very strictly.

'Children should be seen and not heard' was one of her favourite sayings, and 'Speak when you're spoken to' was another. She taught them to say 'Please' and 'Thank you', to eat nicely, to sniff quietly if their noses were running, and never to scratch in public, no matter how many fleas they had.

Six of them – three boys and three girls – grew up to be well behaved, with beautiful manners, but the seventh was a great worry to Hylda and her husband Herbert. This seventh hedgepiglet was indeed the despair of Hylda's life. He was not only seen but constantly heard, speaking whether he was spoken to or not, and he never said 'Please' or 'Thank you'. He gobbled his food in a revolting slobbery way, he sniffed very loudly indeed, and he was forever scratching.

His real name was Norton, but he was more often known as Norty.

Now some mother animals can wallop their young ones if they do not do what they are told. A lioness can cuff her cub, a monkey can clip its child round the ear, or an elephant can give her baby a biff with her trunk. But it's not so easy for hedgehogs.

'Sometimes,' said Hylda to Herbert, 'I wish that hedgepigs didn't have prickles.'

'Why is that, my dear?' said Herbert.

'Because then I could give our Norty a good hiding. He deserves it.'

'Why is that, my dear?' said Herbert.

'Not only is he disobedient, he has taken to answering me back. Why can't he be good like the others? Never have I known such a hedgepiglet. I shall be glad when November comes.'

'Why is that, my dear?' said Herbert.

Hylda sighed. Conversation with my husband, she said to herself for the umpteenth time, can hardly be called interesting.

'Because then it's time to hibernate, of course, and we can all have a good sleep. For five blissful months I shall not have to listen to that impudent, squeaky, little voice arguing, complaining, refusing to do what I say and generally giving me cheek.'

Hylda should have known it would not be that easy.

When November came, she said to her husband and the seven children, 'Come along, all of you.'

'Yes, Mummy,' said the three good boys and the three good girls, and, 'Why is that, my dear?' said Herbert, but Norty only said, 'Shan't.'

'Norty,' said Hylda. 'If you do not do

what you are told, I shall get your father to give you a good hard smack.'

Norty fluffed up his spines and sniggered.

'You'll be sorry if you do, Dad,' he said.

'Where are we going, Mummy?' asked one of the hedgepiglets.

'We are going to find a nice deep bed of dry leaves, where we can hibernate.'

'What does "hibernate" mean, Mummy?' asked another.

'It means to go to sleep, all through

the winter. When it's rainy and blowy and frosty and snowy outside, we shall all be fast asleep under the leaf pile, all cosy and warm. Won't that be lovely?'

'No,' said Norty.

'Norton!' said his mother angrily. 'Are you coming or are you not?'

'No,' said Norty.

'Oh well, stay here then,' snapped Hylda, 'and freeze to death!' and she trotted off with the rest.

In a far corner of the garden they found a nice deep bed of dry leaves, and Hylda and Herbert and the six good hedgepiglets burrowed their way into it, and curled up tight, and shut their eyes, and went to sleep.

The following April they woke up, and opened their eyes, and uncurled, and burrowed out into the spring sunshine.

'Goodbye, Mummy. Goodbye, Daddy,' chorused the six good hedgepiglets, and off they trotted to seek their fortunes.

'Oh, Herbert,' said Hylda. 'I feel so sad.'

'Why is that, my dear?' said Herbert.

'I should never have left our Norty out in the cold last November. He will have frozen to death, poor little fellow. What does it matter that he was rude and disobedient and cheeky? Oh, if only I could hear his squeaky voice again, I'd be the happiest hedgepig ever!'

At that moment there was a rustling from the other side of the bed of leaves, and out came Norty.

'Can't you keep your voices down?' he said, yawning. 'A fellow can't get a wink of sleep.'

'Norty!' cried Hylda. 'You did hibernate, after all!'

'Course I did,' said Norty. 'What did you expect me to do – freeze to death?'

'Oh, my Norty boy!' said Hylda. 'Are you all right?'

'I was,' said Norty, 'till you woke me, nattering on as usual.'

'Now, now,' said Hylda, controlling herself with difficulty, 'that's not the way to speak to your mother, is it? Come here and give me a kiss.'

'Don't want to,' said Norty.

'Anyone would think,' said Hylda, 'that you weren't pleased to see us.'

'Anyone,' said Norty, 'would be right.'

'Well, push off then!' shouted Hylda. 'Your brothers and sisters have all gone, so get lost!'

'Shan't,' said Norty.

He yawned again, full in his mother's face.

'I'm going back to bed,' he said. 'So there.'

At this Hylda completely lost her temper.

'I've had enough!' she screamed. 'You're the rudest hedgepig in the world and your father's the most boring, and I never want to see either of you again!' and she ran away as fast as she could go.

Herbert and Norty stared after her.

Norty scratched his fleas and sniffed very noisily.

'Looks like she's done a bunk, Dad,' he said.

'Yes,' said Herbert. 'Why is that, my dear?'

'Can't think,' said Norty. 'But then she always was prickly.'

The Clockwork Mouse

It really looked very much like a mouse.

Its round ears, its beady black eyes, its whiskers, its long thin tail, and especially its coat of greyish-brown hair were all so life-like. You would have thought it was a real live mouse, until you saw the round hole in its left side. That was the keyhole, and when you wound the mouse up with the little brass key, it scuttled across the room.

Jimmy had been given it for his seventh birthday, and at first he'd had a lot of fun with his clockwork mouse.

He'd frightened the life out of his big sister without even winding it up – he'd just put it quietly on her pillow so that when she woke, she was staring straight at it.

He'd let it run across the carpet just as his mother came into the sitting-room,

and she'd taken a huge jump right into an armchair.

And as for a bossy lady who came to tea and wouldn't stop talking, when the mouse ran straight at her feet, she stopped quick enough and started screaming instead, besides spilling hot tea in her lap, which made her hop about like a jumping jack.

Even the cat was fooled at first and

was about to pounce upon the clockwork mouse, so life-like was it.

But as time passed, everyone became used to Jimmy's toy, and he became bored with it, and, anyway, he lost the key.

So for many years now the clockwork mouse had lain at the bottom of the toy cupboard, gathering dust, until one day Jimmy's mother decided to have a clear-out and get rid of all the children's old toys.

She was packing them into a big cardboard box to take to Oxfam – dolls and model cars and jigsaws and board games and bits of Lego – when she came across the clockwork mouse. For a split second she thought it was a real one as it stared at her with its beady black eyes, and she went cold with sudden fright. But then she recognized it, and picked it up by its tail, holding it rather gingerly between her finger and thumb for the tail felt horribly real.

No key, she thought, Jimmy must have

lost it, so the thing's no use to anyone, and she dropped it into the waste-paper basket.

In due course the basket was emptied into the dustbin, and later the bin men came and tipped the contents of the dustbin into the refuse lorry. Possibly because it was small, the clockwork mouse escaped being squashed by the crusher inside the lorry, and so ended up all in one piece on the rubbish dump.

It rained that afternoon and washed all the dust and dirt off the toy, so that by nightfall it looked as good as new. Once again it looked life-like. So much so that later that night a scavenging fox, searching the dump for food scraps, picked it up in its jaws and carried it off.

At the edge of the field in which the rubbish was being dumped was a wood. In amongst the trees went the fox, mouse in mouth, and then dropped it on the ground. It was a young fox, not much more than a cub, but old enough to realize that this thing that looked like a mouse did not smell or feel like one, so it played with it for a while, tossing it up in the air, and then left it and padded off.

Hours later a little woodmouse, scuttling along through the leaf litter, came suddenly face to face with the toy. Coyly she touched noses with this handsome

stranger, but then her mate appeared and rushed angrily at the clockwork mouse, bowling it over and biting furiously at it.

At that moment the quavering, eerie call of a tawny owl rang out, and the woodmice vanished. Seconds later the owl came swooping low on silent wings and, seeing a motionless mouse, snatched it up and flew off with it. The three hungry owlets waiting in their nest in a hollow tree opened their beaks wide as they saw their mother approach, carrying food, but then they hissed angrily when they found they could not eat the strange, hard object she had brought, so she tossed it out of the nest-hole and flew off again.

The clockwork mouse lay at the foot of the hollow tree for months, until autumn came and the leaves fell and hid it from sight, forgotten by all the world. Only once was it remembered and that was because Jimmy's mother decided to have the old carpet in his bedroom replaced, and the carpet fitter found

something wedged in a crack in the floor-
boards.

'D'you know what this fits, Jimmy?'
his mother said to him later, handing him
a little brass key.

Jimmy looked at it and shook his
head. But then he said, 'Wait a minute
though. I remember now. It's the key to
my clockwork mouse. Where is it, Mum?'

'I chucked it away, years and years ago.'

'Mum! It was my mouse!'

'Honestly, Jimmy,' his mother said,
'anyone would think you were still seven,
instead of twice that age.'

'I liked that mouse,' Jimmy said. 'I
shall keep the key anyway, in memory of
the poor old chap.'

In fact, the poor old chap was on the
move again.

A grey squirrel, searching through the
bed of leaves on the floor of the wood,
trying to remember where it had buried
an acorn, had come upon the clockwork
mouse and scratched at it angrily, kicking

it out into the open.

In the days that followed, a number of other woodland creatures came upon the mouse.

A badger picked it up in its great jaws and carried it a little way and dropped it again.

A weasel worried at it for a moment before tossing it aside.

A hedgehog nibbled at its fur and

found it tasteless.

A green woodpecker tapped it on the head with its strong beak.

And finally a magpie, nosiest of birds, carried it up to its nest of sticks in the top of an ash tree. The magpie, who liked bright things, had been attracted by the gleam in the beady black eyes of the toy, and the clockwork mouse spent the rest of that year in the magpie's nest, along with three bottle-tops, some pieces of coloured glass and a Coca-Cola can.

During the last part of the winter there were some severe gales, and in one of them the ash blew down. For many more months the clockwork mouse lay patiently among the tangle of fallen branches, until one day men came with chain-saws to cut up the tree.

'Look!' said one to another as they worked amid the lop and top. 'Here's a big bird's nest still in one piece. All sorts of rubbish in it too, and what's this? A mouse!'

'A live one, d'you mean?' said the other man.

'I thought it was for a minute,' said the woodcutter. 'Ever so life-like it is. But no, it's a clockwork mouse, would you believe it? See, here's the keyhole in the left side of it. How in the world did it ever get here?' and he stuffed it in his pocket.

'I've ordered a load of logs,' said Jimmy's father next day as he left for work. 'They should be delivered this morning. Some chaps have been cutting up a tree that was blown down in the wood next to the field where the rubbish dump used to be: before they filled it in and landscaped it, remember?'

'I've got to go out,' Jimmy's mother said.

'I'll be here,' said Jimmy. 'I'm not going to school today. I'm revising. I'll see to the logs.'

Later, when the woodcutter had unloaded the logs, Jimmy held out the

money his father had left with him.

'Half a tick,' said the woodcutter.
'There'll be a bit of change out of that,'

and he put his hand in his pocket and brought out some coins, and with them something else.

'Look at this,' he said, and he put the clockwork mouse down on the bed of the pick-up truck.

Jimmy looked.

'Where did you find that?' he said.

'You'll never believe this,' the woodcutter said, 'but that was in a bird's nest, a nest that had been in the top of the ash tree we cut these logs from. It's a clockwork mouse, see? No good to me – I haven't got any kids. And it's no good to you. Got any little brothers?'

'No,' said Jimmy, 'but you can leave it with me if you like.'

The woodcutter laughed.

'OK,' he said, 'you're welcome to it. But it's no use without a key,' and he handed over the toy and drove off.

Jimmy stood holding the clockwork mouse.

'You couldn't be, not after all these

years, could you?' he said, and then he thought – there's only one way to prove it's my mouse.

He fetched the little brass key and put it into the hole in the left side. It fitted! But it wouldn't turn.

'You must be terribly rusty,' said Jimmy, and he fetched the oil can he used on his bicycle and squirted some into the keyhole.

'Now then,' he said. 'Let's see if there's life in the old mouse yet,' and he began to wind. The mechanism was very stiff, but the key turned, just, and at last it was fully wound.

Then Jimmy set his old clockwork mouse on the floor, and slowly, noisily, jerkily it began to move across the carpet.

The passage of time had indeed aged it a great deal. Wind and weather had turned its coat a dirty yellow colour and the hair on it was patchy. Also it had run the gauntlet of a good many animals: one ear was weasel-chewed, its body bore assorted toothmarks, an owlet had taken off part of its tail, and there was a dent in the top of its head where the woodpecker had pecked it.

When it came to a halt, Jimmy picked it up and looked into its beady black eyes.

'I bet you could tell a story,' he said. 'I wonder whatever happened to you.'

The clockwork mouse stared back impassively.

The Happiest Woodlouse

Walter was a wimp. He was scared of his own shadow – always had been since he was tiny.

No matter that he was now a really big woodlouse, with fourteen strong legs and a fine coat of armour, Walter was still afraid of everything and anything. Spiders, black beetles, centipedes, earwigs – whatever kind of creature he met frightened the life out of him, so that he rolled himself into a ball and wouldn't unroll again for ages.

Even with other woodlice he was just the same. Every time he met one, he rolled up and stayed rolled up until the patter of fourteen feet had died away in the distance.

You can easily understand why Walter had no friends.

I would like to make a friend, he said to himself. I would like to be able to have a good chat with someone, crack a joke or two perhaps. It must be nice to have a pal. If only I wasn't so nervous.

At that moment he heard someone approaching the large flat stone under which he was sheltering, and hastily he curled himself into a ball. The footsteps came nearer, and suddenly, to his horror, Walter felt himself being nudged. It was the sort of hefty nudge, Walter thought, that some fierce creature might give a wretched woodlouse before picking it up and swallowing it whole.

But then he heard a voice. It was a jolly voice which did not sound fierce but friendly.

'Wakey! Wakey!' said the voice. 'What's a chap like you doing all curled up on a nice sunny day like this, eh?'

Could this be the friend I've been waiting for, thought Walter?

'What are you?' he said, in somewhat muffled tones, for it is hard to speak clearly when you are curled up in a ball.

'I'm a woodlouse of course, like you,' said the voice. 'Come on, unroll, why don't you? Anyone would think you were afraid of something.'

If you only knew, said Walter to himself, I'm afraid of everything, but all the same he unrolled, to find himself face to face with a woodlouse of about his own size, but of a slightly different colour. Walter was slaty-grey. This stranger was paler, sort of brownish in fact, and freckled all over.

Walter waved his antennae.

'Hello,' he said. 'I'm Walter.'

'Hi,' said the stranger, waving back.

He looks a decent sort of chap, thought Walter. Well, it's now or never, so he took a deep breath and said, 'Will you be my friend?'

'My!' said the freckly stranger. 'You're a fast worker!'

'How do you mean?' said Walter.

'You don't waste time, do you? No remarks about the weather, no polite chit-chat, just "Will you be my friend?" Fair takes a girl's breath away!'

A girl, thought Walter! I just wanted a pal to have a chat with and crack a joke, but a girlfriend! Oh no, I'm frightened of girls. He was just about to curl up again when the stranger said, 'OK.'

Walter hesitated.

'OK what?' he said.

'OK, I'll be your friend, Walter. I've seen worse-looking woodlice than you. By the way, my name's Marilyn.'

'Oh,' said Walter.

He wiggled several pairs of legs nervously.

'I'm pleased to meet you,' he said.

'You're a funny boy,' said Marilyn with a light laugh, and she moved forward until her antennae brushed gently against his.

At this touch something like an electric shock ran through every plate of Walter's armour and he found himself suddenly very short of breath.

'Come on,' said Marilyn. 'Let's go for a stroll.'

Ordinarily Walter never came out from beneath his large flat stone till nightfall. Spiders and black beetles and centipedes and earwigs were frightening enough, but in daylight, out in the open, there was far worse danger. Birds! Birds with sharp eyes and sharper beaks that snapped up spiders and black beetles and centipedes and earwigs – and woodlice!

'Can't we wait till after dark, Marilyn?' he said.

Marilyn giggled.

'Oh, you are a one!' she said, and out she went and off along the garden path.

Despite himself, Walter followed. He

was frightened, terrified indeed, but he hurried after Marilyn as fast as his seven pairs of legs could carry him. How beautiful she was, he now could see. Her long antennae, the slender legs, each delicate joint of her freckled carapace – all were perfection. Here, in the wide open spaces of the garden, death might threaten, but without Marilyn, thought Walter, life would not be worth living.

'Wait for me!' he called, but even as he spoke he saw to his horror that in the middle of the path ahead there squatted a huge slimy monster.

'Marilyn!' he cried. 'Watch out!' and hastily he rolled himself into a ball. Miserably he waited, tightly curled. Cruel Fate, thought Walter. I meet the love of my life and within minutes she walks down a monster's throat. If only I were brave, I might have tackled the brute. But I'm not, alas, I'm not.

Then a voice said, 'Are you coming, Walter, or aren't you?'

'What were you playing at?' said Marilyn when, sheepishly, he caught up with her. Of the monster there was no sign but a trail of slime across the flagstones.

Walter gulped.

'I thought I saw a monster,' he said.

'Monster?' said Marilyn. 'That was only an old slug. Mind where you're putting your feet, the path's all sticky.'

They walked on, off the path and on to a rose-bed under whose bushes was a scattering of dead leaves. On these they began to browse, side by side.

'Walter,' said Marilyn.

'Yes, Marilyn?'

'You've got a yellow streak, haven't you?'

Walter did not answer.

'Not to mince words,' said Marilyn, 'you're a chicken-hearted scaredy-cat and a cowardy-custard, aren't you?'

'Yes,' said Walter.

'Well, at least you've been honest with me,' said Marilyn, 'so I'll do the same for

you. Let's just forget the friendship bit. You're a nice boy, but if there's one thing I can't stand, it's a wimp. No hard feelings, eh?'

'But, Marilyn . . .' said Walter.

'Yes?'

'I . . . I love you.'

For a moment Marilyn gazed thoughtfully at Walter. Such a good-looking fellow, but no backbone. Shame, really.

'Sorry, Walter,' she said. 'See you around, maybe,' and she turned to go.

As she did so, Walter saw the thrush come hopping through the rose-bed, straight towards her.

Even as he tensed his muscles to roll himself into a ball, something snapped in his brain, and instead he rushed forward on his fourteen powerful legs.

'Roll up, quick!' he shouted at Marilyn, shoving her out of his way, and then, as instinctively she obeyed, Walter made directly for the huge bird.

'Take me!' he cried. 'Take me, you brute, but spare my Marilyn!'

The thrush put its head on one side,

the better to focus upon this foolhardy woodlouse, when it saw from the corner of its other eye a fat worm. Leaving Walter for afters, it picked up the worm and swallowed it.

As it was doing so, a large tabby cat came strolling down the garden path, waving its tail, and the thrush flew hastily away.

'All clear!' cried Walter, and Marilyn unrolled.

'You saved my life!' she breathed.

'Well, I don't know about that,' said Walter in an embarrassed voice.

'Well, you jolly well tried to,' said Marilyn. 'You were ready to sacrifice yourself to protect me, weren't you?'

'Yes,' said Walter.

Marilyn stared at her gallant knight in armour.

To think, she said to herself, that I called him a cowardy-custard. Her heart swelled within her bosom, and she went weak at the knees, all fourteen of them.

'Oh Walter,' she said softly, 'I am yours, all yours.'

'Oh Marilyn,' said Walter. 'You have made me the happiest woodlouse in the world!'

Use Your Brains

Little Basil Brontosaurus came home from his first morning at playschool in floods of tears.

'Whatever's the matter, darling?' said his mother, whose name was Araminta. 'Why are you crying?'

'They've been teasing me,' sobbed Basil.

'Who have? The other children?'

A variety of little dinosaurs went to

the playschool. There were diplodocuses, iguanodons, ankylosauruses and many others. Basil was the only young bronto-saurus.

'Yes,' sniffed Basil. 'They said I was stupid. They said I hadn't got a brain in my head.'

At this point Basil's father, a forty-ton brontosaurus who measured eighty feet from nose to tail-tip, came lumbering up through the shallows of the lake in which the family lived.

'Herb!' called Araminta. 'Did you hear that? The kids at playschool said our Basil hadn't a brain in his head.'

Herb considered this while pulling up and swallowing large quantities of water-weed.

'He has,' he said at last. 'Hasn't he?'

'Of course you have, darling,' said Araminta to her little son. 'Come along with me now, and dry your tears and listen carefully.'

Still snivelling, Basil waded into the

lake and followed his mother to a secluded inlet, well away from the other dinosaurs that were feeding around the shallows.

Araminta settled herself where the water was deep enough to help support her enormous bulk.

'Now listen to Mummy, Basil darling,' she said. 'What I'm about to tell you is a secret. Every brontosaurus that ever hatched is told this secret by his or her mummy or daddy, once he or she is old enough. One day you'll be grown up, and you'll have a wife of your own, and she'll lay eggs, and then you'll have babies. And when those babies are old enough, they'll have to be told, just like I'm going to tell you.'

'Tell me what?' said Basil.

'Promise not to breathe a word of it to the other children?'

'All right. But what is it?'

'It is this,' said Araminta. 'We have two brains.'

'You're joking,' said Basil.

'I'm not. Every brontosaurus has two brains. One in its head and one in the middle of its back.'

'Wow!' cried Basil. 'Well, if I've got two brains and all the other kids have only got one, I must be twice as clever as them.'

'You are, darling,' said Araminta. 'You are. So let's have no more of this cry-baby nonsense. Next time one of the children teases you, just think to yourself "I am twice as clever as you".'

Not only did Basil think this, next morning at playschool, but he also thought that he was twice as big as the other children.

'Did you have a nice time?' said Araminta, when he came home.

'Smashing,' said Basil.

'No tears?'

'Not mine,' said Basil cheerily.

'You didn't tell anyone our secret?'

'Oh no,' said Basil. 'I didn't do much talking to the other kids. Actions speak louder than words.'

Not long after this the playschool teacher, an elderly female stegosaurus, came to see Herb and Araminta.

'I'm sorry to bother you,' she said, 'but I'm a little worried about Basil.'

'Not been blubbing again, has he?' said Herb.

'Oh no, *he* hasn't,' said the stegosaurus. 'In fact, recently he has grown greatly in confidence. At first he was rather nervous and the other children tended to make fun of him, but they don't any more. Something seems to have given him a great deal of self-assurance. He's twice the boy he was.'

'Can't think why,' said Herb, but Araminta could.

'Indeed,' went on the stegosaurus, 'I fear that lately he's been throwing his weight about. Boys will be boys, I know, but really Basil has become very rough. Only yesterday I had to send home a baby brachiosaurus with a badly bruised foot and a little trachodon with a black eye. I should be glad if you would speak to Basil about all this.'

When the teacher had departed, Araminta said to Herb, 'You must have a word with the boy.'

'Why?' said Herb.

'You heard what the teacher said. He's been bullying the other children. He's obviously getting above himself.'

At this point Basil appeared.

'What did old Steggy want?' he said.

'Tell him, Herb,' said Araminta.

'Now look here, my boy,' said Herb.

Basil looked.

'You listen to me.'

Basil listened, but Herb, Araminta could see, had lost the thread of the matter.

'Your father is very angry with you,' she said. 'You have been fighting. At play-school.'

'That's right,' said Herb. 'Fighting. At playschool. Why?'

'Well, it's like this, Dad,' said Basil. 'The first day, the other kids teased me. They said I hadn't got a brain in my head, remember? And then Mum told me I had. And another in the middle of my back. Two brains! So I thought I'm twice as clever as the rest as well as twice as big, so why not lean on them a bit? Not my fault if they get under my feet.'

'You want to watch your step,' said Herb.

'Daddy's right,' said Araminta. 'One of these days you'll get into real trouble. Now run along, I want to talk to your father.'

'It's all my fault for telling him about having two brains,' she said when Basil had gone. 'He's too young. My parents didn't tell me till I was nearly grown-up. How did you find out?'

'Oh, I don't know,' said Herb. 'I dare say I heard some of the chaps talking.

Down in the swamp. When I was one of the gang. We used to talk a lot, down in the swamp.'

'What about?' said Araminta.

'Water-weed, mostly,' said Herb, and he pulled up a great mouthful and began to chomp.

Not long after this, Basil was expelled.

'I'm sorry,' said the elderly stegosaurus, 'but I can't have the boy in my class any longer. It isn't only his roughness, it's his rudeness. Do you know what he said to me today?'

'No,' said Herb.

'What?' said Araminta.

'He said to me "I'm twice as clever as you are".'

'Is he?' said Herb.

'Of course he isn't,' said Araminta hastily. 'He was just being silly and childish. I'm sure he won't be any trouble in the future.'

'Not in my playschool he won't,' said

the stegosaurus and then, oddly, she used the very words that Araminta had used earlier.

'One of these days,' she said, 'he'll get into real trouble,' and off she waddled, flapping her plates angrily.

And one of those days, Basil did.

Being expelled from playschool hadn't worried him at all. What do I want with other dinosaurs, he thought. I'm far superior to them, with my two brains, one to work my neck and my front legs, one to work my back legs and my tail. Brontosauruses are twice as clever as other dinosaurs and I'm twice as clever as any other brontosaurus.

You couldn't say that Basil was bigheaded for that was almost the smallest part of him, but you could certainly say that he was boastful, conceited and arrogant.

'That boy!' said Araminta to Herb. 'He's boastful, conceited and arrogant.

He must get it from your side of the family, swaggering about and picking fights all the time. What does he think he is? A tyrannosaurus rex?'

'What do you think you are?' Basil was saying at that very moment. He had come out of the lake where the family spent almost all their time, and set off for a walk.

He was ambling along, thinking what a fine fellow he was, when he suddenly saw a strange, smallish dinosaur standing in his path.

It was not like any dinosaur he had ever seen before. It stood upright on its hind legs which were much bigger than its little forelegs, and it had a large head with large jaws and a great many teeth. But compared to Basil, who already weighed a couple of tons, it looked quite small, and he advanced upon it, saying in a rude tone, 'What do you think you are?'

'I'm a tyrannosaurus rex,' said the stranger.

'Never heard of you,' said Basil.

'Lucky you.'

'Why? What's so wonderful about you? You can't even walk on four feet like a decent dinosaur and you've only got one brain. You'll be telling me next that you don't eat water-weed like we do.'

'We don't,' said the other. 'We only eat meat.'

'What sort of meat?'

'Brontosaurus, mostly.'

'Let's get this straight,' said Basil. 'Are you seriously telling me that you kill brontosauruses and eat them?'

'Yes.'

'Don't make me laugh,' said Basil. 'I'm four times as big as you.'

'Yes,' said the youngster, 'but my dad's four times as big as you. Oh look, what a bit of luck, here he comes!'

Basil looked up to see a terrifying sight.

Marching towards him on its huge

hind legs was a towering, full-grown tyrannosaurus rex. In its forepaws it held the remains of the body of some wretched smaller dinosaur, from which it tore mouthfuls with its battery of six-inch teeth. Blood dripped from its mighty jaws as it chewed and swallowed, and all of a sudden Basil had two brainwaves.

Time I went, he thought. Sharpish. And as one brain sent a message rippling along to the other, he turned tail and made for the safety of the lake as fast as his legs could carry him.

Like all his kind, he was slow and clumsy on land, and if his pursuer had not recently made a kill, Basil must surely have been its next victim.

As it was, he reached the shore of the lake in time and splashed frantically out to deeper water, where his parents, their long necks downstretched, were browsing on the weedy bottom.

Araminta was the first to look up.

'Hello, darling,' she said. 'Where have

you been? Whatever's the matter? You're all of a doodah.'

'Oh Mummy, Mummy!' panted Basil. 'It was awful! I went for a walk and I was nearly eaten by a tyrannosaurus rex!'

Herb raised his head in time to hear this.

'That'll teach you,' he said.

'Teach me what, Dad?'

'Not to be so cocky,' said Araminta.

'Ever since I told you that secret you've been unbearable, Basil. I hope this will be a lesson to you.'

'Oh, it will, Mummy, it will!' cried Basil. 'I won't ever shoot my mouth off again.'

'And don't go for walks,' said his mother, 'but keep close to the lake where you'll be safe from the tyrannosaurus.'

'In case he rex you,' said Herb and plunged his head underwater again, while strings of bubbles rose as he laughed at his own joke.

'And if you want to grow up to be as big as your father,' said Araminta, 'there's one thing you must always remember to do.'

'What's that, Mummy?' said Basil.

'Use your brains.'

READ MORE IN PUFFIN

For children of all ages, Puffin represents quality and variety – the very best in publishing today around the world.

For complete information about books available from Puffin – and Penguin – and how to order them, contact us at the appropriate address below. Please note that for copyright reasons the selection of books varies from country to country.

On the worldwide web: www.puffin.co.uk

In the United Kingdom: Please write to *Dept. EP, Penguin Books Ltd, Bath Road, Harmondsworth, West Drayton, Middlesex UB7 ODA*

In the United States: Please write to *Consumer Sales, Penguin USA, P.O. Box 999, Dept. 17109, Bergenfield, New Jersey 07621-0120*. VISA and MasterCard holders call 1-800-253-6476 to order Penguin titles

In Canada: Please write to *Penguin Books Canada Ltd, 10 Alcorn Avenue, Suite 300, Toronto, Ontario M4V 3B2*

In Australia: Please write to *Penguin Books Australia Ltd, P.O. Box 257, Ringwood, Victoria 3134*

In New Zealand: Please write to *Penguin Books (NZ) Ltd, Private Bag 102902, North Shore Mail Centre, Auckland 10*

In India: Please write to *Penguin Books India Pvt Ltd, 706 Eros Apartments, 56 Nehru Place, New Delhi 110 019*

In the Netherlands: Please write to *Penguin Books Netherlands bv, Postbus 3507, NL-1001 AH Amsterdam*

In Germany: Please write to *Penguin Books Deutschland GmbH, Metzlerstrasse 26, 60594 Frankfurt am Main*

In Spain: Please write to *Penguin Books S. A., Bravo Murillo 19, 1° B, 28015 Madrid*

In Italy: Please write to *Penguin Italia s.r.l., Via Felice Casati 20, I–20124 Milano*

In France: Please write to *Penguin France S. A., 17 rue Lejeune, F–31000 Toulouse*

In Japan: Please write to *Penguin Books Japan, Ishikiribashi Building, 2–5–4, Suido, Bunkyo-ku, Tokyo 112*

In South Africa: Please write to *Longman Penguin Southern Africa (Pty) Ltd, Private Bag X08, Bertsham 2013*